High Time for Heroes

Magic Tree House® Books

#1: DINOSAURS BEFORE DARK
#2: THE KNIGHT AT DAWN
#3: MUMMIES IN THE MORNING
#4: PIRATES PAST NOON
#5: NIGHT OF THE NINJAS
#6: AFTERNOON ON THE AMAZON
#7: SUNSET OF THE SABERTOOTH
#8: MIDNIGHT ON THE MOON
#9: DOLPHINS AT DAYBREAK
#10: GHOST TOWN AT SUNDOWN
#11: LIONS AT LUNCHTIME
#12: POLAR BEARS PAST BEDTIME
#13: VACATION UNDER THE VOLCANO
#14: DAY OF THE DRAGON KING
#15: VIKING SHIPS AT SUNRISE
#16: HOUR OF THE OLYMPICS
#17: TONIGHT ON THE *TITANIC*
#18: BUFFALO BEFORE BREAKFAST
#19: TIGERS AT TWILIGHT
#20: DINGOES AT DINNERTIME
#21: CIVIL WAR ON SUNDAY
#22: REVOLUTIONARY WAR
    ON WEDNESDAY
#23: TWISTER ON TUESDAY
#24: EARTHQUAKE IN THE
    EARLY MORNING
#25: STAGE FRIGHT ON A
    SUMMER NIGHT
#26: GOOD MORNING, GORILLAS
#27: THANKSGIVING ON THURSDAY
#28: HIGH TIDE IN HAWAII

Merlin Missions

#29: CHRISTMAS IN CAMELOT
#30: HAUNTED CASTLE ON HALLOWS EVE
#31: SUMMER OF THE SEA SERPENT
#32: WINTER OF THE ICE WIZARD
#33: CARNIVAL AT CANDLELIGHT
#34: SEASON OF THE SANDSTORMS
#35: NIGHT OF THE NEW MAGICIANS
#36: BLIZZARD OF THE BLUE MOON
#37: DRAGON OF THE RED DAWN
#38: MONDAY WITH A MAD GENIUS
#39: DARK DAY IN THE DEEP SEA
#40: EVE OF THE EMPEROR PENGUIN
#41: MOONLIGHT ON THE MAGIC FLUTE
#42: A GOOD NIGHT FOR GHOSTS

#43: LEPRECHAUN IN LATE WINTER
#44: A GHOST TALE FOR CHRISTMAS TIME
#45: A CRAZY DAY WITH COBRAS
#46: DOGS IN THE DEAD OF NIGHT
#47: ABE LINCOLN AT LAST!
#48: A PERFECT TIME FOR PANDAS
#49: STALLION BY STARLIGHT
#50: HURRY UP, HOUDINI!

Magic Tree House® Fact Trackers

DINOSAURS
KNIGHTS AND CASTLES
MUMMIES AND PYRAMIDS
PIRATES
RAIN FORESTS
SPACE
TITANIC
TWISTERS AND OTHER TERRIBLE STORMS
DOLPHINS AND SHARKS
ANCIENT GREECE AND THE OLYMPICS
AMERICAN REVOLUTION
SABERTOOTHS AND THE ICE AGE
PILGRIMS
ANCIENT ROME AND POMPEII
TSUNAMIS AND OTHER NATURAL DISASTERS
POLAR BEARS AND THE ARCTIC
SEA MONSTERS
PENGUINS AND ANTARCTICA
LEONARDO DA VINCI
GHOSTS
LEPRECHAUNS AND IRISH FOLKLORE
RAGS AND RICHES: KIDS IN THE TIME OF
    CHARLES DICKENS
SNAKES AND OTHER REPTILES
DOG HEROES
ABRAHAM LINCOLN
PANDAS AND OTHER ENDANGERED SPECIES
HORSE HEROES
HEROES FOR ALL TIMES

More Magic Tree House®

GAMES AND PUZZLES FROM THE TREE HOUSE
MAGIC TRICKS FROM THE TREE HOUSE

MAGIC TREE HOUSE® #51
A MERLIN MISSION

High Time
for Heroes

by Mary Pope Osborne

illustrated by Sal Murdocca

A STEPPING STONE BOOK™

Random House 🏠 New York

For Paul Aiken,
one of my heroes

Visit us on the Web!
randomhouse.com/kids
MagicTreeHouse.com

Educators and librarians, for a variety of teaching tools, visit us at
RHTeachersLibrarians.com

Library of Congress Cataloging-in-Publication Data
Osborne, Mary Pope.
High time for heroes / Mary Pope Osborne ; jacket art and interior illustrations, Sal Murdocca. — First edition.
   pages cm. — (A stepping stone book [tm]) (Magic Tree House ; #51)
Summary: Jack and Annie are magically transported to mid-1800's Thebes where they are saved from a dangerous accident by Florence Nightingale!
ISBN 978-0-307-98049-6 (trade) — ISBN 978-0-307-98050-2 (lib. bdg.) —
ISBN 978-0-307-98051-9 (ebook)
[1. Time travel—Fiction. 2. Magicians—Fiction. 3. Nightingale, Florence, 1820–1910—Fiction. 4. Nurses—Fiction. 5. Tree houses—Fiction. 6. Thebes (Egypt : Extinct city)—Fiction.] I. Murdocca, Sal, illustrator. II. Title.
PZ7.O81167Hj 2014   [Fic]—dc23   2013019148

Printed in the United States of America
10 9 8 7 6 5 4 3 2
First Edition

CONTENTS

Prologue

One summer day in Frog Creek, Pennsylvania, a mysterious tree house appeared in the woods. It was filled with books. A boy named Jack and his sister, Annie, found the tree house and soon discovered that it was magic. They could go to any time and place in history just by pointing to a picture in one of the books. While they were gone, no time at all passed back in Frog Creek.

Jack and Annie eventually found out that the tree house belonged to Morgan le Fay, a magical librarian from the legendary realm of Camelot. They have since traveled on many adventures in the magic tree house and completed many missions for both Morgan le Fay and her friend Merlin the magician.

Now Merlin needs Jack and Annie's help again. He wants them to travel through time and learn four secrets of greatness from people who are called great by the world. Jack and Annie have completed two of the four missions. They took a trip to ancient Macedonia, where they spent time with Alexander the Great and his warhorse, Bucephalus, and they visited Coney Island in 1908, where they saw Harry Houdini and his wife, Bess, perform a magic show.

Back in Frog Creek, they are waiting to see where Merlin will send them to find the next secret of greatness. . . .

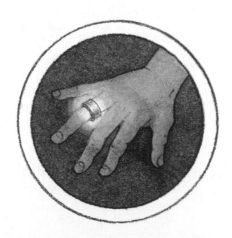

CHAPTER ONE

I Know Her!

J ack sat in a sunny spot on the front porch, studying a book of magic tricks. He was planning to put on a magic show for his parents and grandparents. He took a sip of lemonade, then started making a list in his notebook:

flying paper clips

"Hey." Annie tapped on the screen door. "Let's do something."

"I'm *already* doing something," said Jack. He

took another sip of lemonade and added more
tricks to his list:

magical clinging pen
great pepper trick

Annie gasped. "Did you hear that?" she asked.
She opened the door and came out onto the porch.

"Hear what?" said Jack. He added another
trick:

steal-the-strength trick

"That *whoosh*ing sound," said Annie.

"*Whoosh*ing sound?" Jack read his list and de-
cided he still needed two or three more tricks.

"Like the tree house just *whoosh*ed into the
woods!" said Annie.

"Yeah, yeah," said Jack. He flipped through
the pages of his book.

"Come on, go with me," Annie pleaded. "Let's
check the woods again. *Please.*"

"We've already checked five times since Tuesday," said Jack.

"Once more won't kill you," said Annie. "I have this feeling . . . I'm serious."

Jack sighed. "Okay. You win," he said. "One more time." He put his notebook and pencil into his backpack. Leaving his book of magic tricks on the porch, he stood up and followed Annie down the steps and across their yard.

"Aren't you dying to find another secret of greatness for Merlin?" Annie asked as they headed up the sidewalk. "And what about the magic mist? Don't you want to have another great talent for an hour?"

"Of course," said Jack. "But I'm also tired of looking for the tree house and not finding it! For two weeks you've had these hunches."

Jack and Annie crossed the street and headed into the Frog Creek woods. Winding through the shadows of trees, Jack took a deep breath, inhaling the scent of warm earth and summer leaves. Hidden birds sang from the tree branches. As Jack and Annie drew closer to the tallest oak, Jack's heart started to pound. This time, something *was* there, high in the branches of the tree.

"*Whoosh,*" Annie said softly.

Jack grinned as he looked up at the small wooden house nestled high in the branches. "Okay," he said. "I'm glad we checked."

Annie ran to the rope ladder and started up. Jack followed. Inside the magic tree house, the shadows of branches danced on the wooden walls. A piece of paper, a gold ring, a tiny bottle, a small book, and a scroll were waiting on the floor.

"A new message from Merlin!" said Annie. She picked up the scroll, unrolled it, and read aloud:

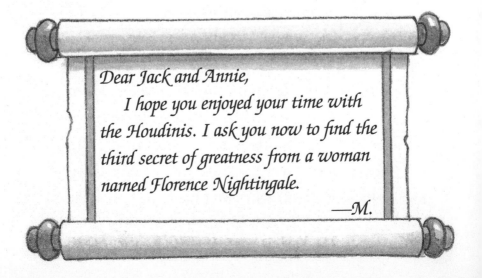

Dear Jack and Annie,
    I hope you enjoyed your time with the Houdinis. I ask you now to find the third secret of greatness from a woman named Florence Nightingale.
                                    —M.

"*Florence Nightingale?*" said Annie. "I know her! I gave a report on her!"

"I just know her name. Who is she?" said Jack.

"She's amazing! She's one of my heroes!" said Annie.

"Yeah, okay, but what did she *do*?" asked Jack.

"Florence Nightingale lived in the 1800s, in England," said Annie. "The English army was fighting in this place called the Crimea, on the Black Sea, and Florence Nightingale was a nurse there. The soldiers called her the Lady with the Lamp, because after the hospital was quiet and dark at night, she went alone from bed to bed with a lantern. She gave light and comfort and took care of wounds. She was so brave and amazing, she became famous everywhere! Later she changed the world of nursing by organizing—"

"Okay, you don't have to give your whole report," Jack interrupted. "I get the picture. She sounds cool. Let's go meet her."

"I feel like I already know her!" said Annie with a laugh. "Oh, wow! I can't wait!"

"So let's see where we're going," said Jack. He picked up the small book from the floor. Its faded leather cover had an old-fashioned look.

"I'll bet it's about England," said Annie, "or the Crimea."

"Neither," said Jack. He showed the cover to Annie:

"Egypt?" said Annie. "I never read that Florence Nightingale was a nurse in Egypt."

"We've been to Egypt before," said Jack. "Remember the mummy in the pyramid?"

"The ghost-queen," said Annie. "She was on her way to the Next Life."

Jack shivered. "That was weird," he said.

"Don't worry. The ghost-queen was thousands of years in the past," said Annie. "Now we're just going to 1850."

"Ohhh . . . right," said Jack drily. "I guess all the ancient ghosts were gone by then."

"Whatever. Ready?" said Annie.

"Hold on," said Jack. He picked up the gold ring and gave it to Annie. "It's your turn to wear this," he said.

Annie slipped the ring onto her finger. They both stared at it for a moment. The ring was magic. When Florence Nightingale shared a secret of greatness with them, it would glow like a burning ember.

"The Ring of Truth," said Annie.

"Yep. Just remember to keep checking it when we're talking to Florence," said Jack.

"Don't worry, I will," said Annie. "Here, you carry this." She picked up the tiny glass bottle and handed it to Jack.

Jack held the bottle up to the dappled sunlight and looked at the silver vapor swirling inside. "Mist gathered at first light on the first day of the new moon on the Isle of Avalon," he said.

"Yep. Good for one hour of great talent," said Annie.

Jack smiled, remembering their hour as horse trainers and their hour as stage magicians. "I wonder what we'll be great at this time," he said.

"Maybe great nurses?" said Annie.

"We'll see," said Jack. He put the tiny bottle in his backpack; then he picked up the piece of paper from the floor. On the paper he had written the two secrets of greatness they'd already learned:

HUMILITY

HARD WORK

"Ready to find the third secret from Florence Nightingale?" he asked.

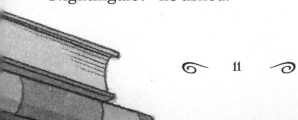

"A thousand times yes!" said Annie.

Jack pointed to the picture on the cover of the *Travelers' Handbook to Egypt.* "I wish we could go there," he said.

The wind started to blow.

The tree house started to spin.

It spun faster and faster.

Then everything was still.

Absolutely still.

CHAPTER TWO

Welcome to Thebes!

Warm, dry air filled the tree house. Jack wore a helmet-type hat, leather boots, a long-sleeved shirt, and a pair of heavy linen pants with a leather belt. A large pouch was attached to the belt.

"I wish I was dressed like you," said Annie, making a face. She was wearing a long white dress with frilly lace. "You look like a cool explorer. I look like I'm going to a tea party."

"Don't feel bad," said Jack. "My clothes are really scratchy and heavy."

HEE-HAW!

"Is that a donkey?" said Annie. She and Jack looked out the window of the tree house. Leaves and branches completely blocked their view.

"I think we landed in a sycamore tree," said Jack, studying the leaves.

Annie pushed some branches aside. All they could see below were more leaves. But straight ahead, in the distance, was a wide plain dotted with sand-colored ruins. Beyond the plain, mountains loomed against a cloudless blue sky. The Egyptian sun was blindingly bright.

HEE-HAW!

"That's definitely a donkey," said Annie. "Let's go look." She gathered up her long white dress and started down the rope ladder.

Jack stuck the small handbook into his leather pouch. He saw that his notebook, his pencil, and the bottle of magic mist were also inside the pouch, along with some coins that showed images of pharaohs. "Hey, we have some Egyptian money!" he called down to Annie.

"Great, come on down!" said Annie. She was already on the ground.

Jack buckled his pouch, then clumsily climbed down the rope ladder in his leather boots. As soon as he stepped onto the grass, flies landed on his face. He shook his head and waved his hands, trying to brush them away.

The sycamore tree was surrounded by bushes and other plants on a lush green riverbank. Across the river, several dozen sailboats were anchored near a temple.

HEE-HAW!

The sound came from beyond the bushes. Jack and Annie stepped around them and peeked out. "Yep, donkeys. Two of them," said Jack. "And there's a little kid with them."

About fifty feet down the river, two small donkeys were standing under a cluster of palm trees. They were shaking their long, furry ears and swishing their tails to keep the flies away. A boy was napping in a rowboat on the riverbank. He wore a striped robe.

"Want to talk to him?" said Annie.

"Sure," said Jack.

They walked out of the bushes and headed toward the boy. "Hello!" Annie called.

The small boy scrambled out of the rowboat. He looked to be only six or seven. "I did not see

you coming," he said. "Welcome to Thebes! My
name is Ali. Do you need donkeys and a guide?"

"No thanks," said Jack.

"My grandfather is the best guide in Thebes,"
Ali said with pride. "He is returning now with

two travelers from England. There he is! On the horse!"

In the distance, a white-bearded man wearing a turban was riding a packhorse. He was leading a man and woman on donkeys toward the river.

"After my grandfather rows them across the Nile to their boat, he can guide you to the tombs in the cliffs!" said Ali. "Or the Temple of Luxor." He pointed to the temple across the river.

"Thanks. Maybe later," said Jack.

"We are here every day. Come back!" said Ali, and he ran to meet his grandfather and the travelers from England.

"We just learned a lot," Jack said to Annie. "It seems we landed in Thebes, Egypt, on the River Nile, across from the Temple of Luxor."

"Sounds like a fairy tale," said Annie.

Jack pulled out their Egypt handbook. He found *Thebes* and read aloud:

Travelers enjoy visiting the area of Thebes in Egypt. Four thousand years ago, the

Egyptian city was the capital of the known world. At that time, it was the noisiest and liveliest place on the River Nile.

"Seriously?" said Jack. He looked around at the quiet riverbank, the donkeys, and the distant bare mountains.

"I guess times have changed for Thebes," said Annie.

"No kidding," said Jack. "So I wonder what Florence Nightingale is doing here."

"Nursing," said Annie. "She has to be! That's what she's famous for. Maybe those English travelers know something about her." Annie pointed to the couple riding with Ali's grandfather. "Remember, Florence was from England, too."

Jack and Annie watched the three riders arrive at the riverbank. Ali's grandfather climbed off his packhorse and helped the couple off their donkeys. As Ali and his grandfather gave the donkeys water, the English woman noticed Jack and Annie. "Hello, children!" she called, waving.

Jack and Annie waved back, and the couple headed toward them. "How delightful to see new faces in Thebes!" the woman said.

"Yes!" said the man, smiling. "Who are you? Where are you from?" The man and woman were both stout and middle-aged, but they had a young, exuberant air about them.

"I'm Annie, and he's my brother, Jack," said Annie. "We're from Frog Creek, Pennsylvania."

"Americans! Wonderful!" said the woman. "We are from England. My name is Selina Bracebridge. I'm traveling with my husband, Charles."

"And I am that very Charles," said Charles. "With whom are you two traveling?"

"Uh . . . our parents," said Annie, "but they left us on our own in Thebes."

"To visit the ruins," said Jack. "They said it would be . . . um . . . a great educational experience."

"What brave American children you are!" Selina said. "And what unusual parents."

"Indeed. And where are you brave American children staying?" asked Charles.

"Uh . . . up the Nile, that way," said Annie. She waved her hand vaguely toward the tree house. "In a little house. It's sort of like an inn."

"I see. Good, good!" said Charles. "Well, can we do anything to help you? With your Thebes educational experience?"

Jack could tell the man was joking, but Annie answered right away. "Actually you *can* help us," she said. "Have either of you heard of a woman named Florence Nightingale? At the place we're staying, someone said she was in Thebes."

Selina's eyes widened in amazement. "Charles, did you hear that? They're looking for Flo!"

Jack looked at Annie, then back at Charles and Selina. "You *know* Florence Nightingale?" he said.

"Know her? She's our best friend!" said Selina. "She's traveling with us, for goodness' sake!" She pointed at the sailboats anchored along the river.

"For many weeks now, she has been sailing up and down the Nile with us in our boat," said Charles.

"That *is* amazing!" Annie said to Jack.

"Totally!" he said.

"How do you two know Flo?" asked Selina.

"Well, we don't exactly *know* her," said Annie. "We just know she's a world-famous nurse."

"A *what*?" said Selina.

"A world-famous . . . nurse?" said Annie. "Like, a nurse in a hospital?"

Charles and Selina both laughed. "Oh, no!" said Selina. "Not Flo! She's helped sick relatives and villagers in their homes. But she's not the least bit famous for that!"

"And she's certainly never worked in a hospital!" said Charles. "I'm afraid you have found the wrong Florence Nightingale."

"Oh," said Jack. *How many Florence Nightingales can there be?* he wondered.

"But your Flo's a great person, right?" Annie said.

"*We* certainly think so!" said Selina.

"Well, then we'd still like to meet her," said Annie.

"Righto!" said Selina. "Flo is visiting the Temple of Luxor this morning. Why don't you come with us to our boat and wait for her to come back?"

"Oh, thank you!" said Annie.

"Excellent!" said Charles. "Mustafa will ferry us across in his rowboat." He turned to the bearded guide and his grandson. "Mustafa, shall we be off?" he called. "Good-bye, Ali!"

The boy waved good-bye, and his grandfather pulled the rowboat partway into the water.

"Children first," said Charles.

Mustafa held the rowboat steady as Jack and Annie climbed aboard and sat down. Then he helped Charles and Selina aboard and climbed in after them.

Once everyone was settled, Mustafa pushed offshore with his oars and started rowing across the Nile. As the boat glided over the sun-sparkling water, the old Egyptian softly sang a song. Jack couldn't understand the words, but the song was soothing, sung in rhythm with the movement of the oars.

"This is perfect," Annie whispered. "Now all we have to do is spend time with Florence

Nightingale and wait for the Ring of Truth to glow."

"Yeah, but she's not a great nurse," whispered Jack, fanning away the flies. "She's not famous for being great at anything."

"I know. That's a little confusing," Annie whispered back.

"Look, children!" said Charles. "Isn't that a magnificent sight?" He pointed to a huge crocodile sunning itself on a river rock.

"Whoa!" said Jack.

"Yikes!" said Annie at the same time. The crocodile had a scaly green hide with black spots. Its green eyes glimmered as the rowboat passed by.

"Don't be alarmed," said Charles. "In our experience, Nile crocodiles are completely harmless."

Harmless? Crocodiles? thought Jack. *I don't think so.*

Mustafa stopped singing as they reached the landing on the opposite riverbank. He climbed out of the rowboat and tied it up. Then he helped Annie and Jack onto the bank. Selina and Charles followed.

Charles handed some money to the guide. "Thank you, Mustafa," he said. "Please wait on this shore, as I believe Miss Nightingale plans to visit western Thebes later today, when it's a bit cooler. This way, children."

Jack and Annie followed Charles and Selina as they walked briskly along the landing, passing the line of sailboats moored at the water's edge. "Whose boats are those?" asked Annie.

"They are rented by travelers from all over Europe," said Charles, "most of whom are hiding from the midday heat right now."

I don't blame them, thought Jack. The heat and the flies were almost more than he could bear. He felt sorry for the workers on the boat decks, scrubbing floors and mending sails.

"Here we are!" said Selina. She and Charles stopped at the largest boat anchored on the river. "Home, sweet home!"

CHAPTER THREE

Beasts on the Nile

"All aboard!" said Charles. The English couple led the way across a short gangplank onto the deck of their sailboat.

The boat had a long cabin and a tall mast with a furled sail. Two crew members in white clothes were mopping the deck. "Miss Selina!" one called. "Lord and Lady Bickerson are waiting inside, to visit with Miss Florence."

"Oh, no! I didn't know *they* were coming," Selina said under her breath.

Charles stopped and stroked his mustache.

"Excuse me, my dear," he said. "But while those particular folk are aboard, I believe I shall take a stroll. Pleasure to meet you, Jack and Annie." He tipped his hat, then retreated back down the gangplank.

"Coward!" called Selina.

Charles turned and saluted her from the riverbank. "Do give my best to the Bickersons, darling! Ta-ta!" he said, and took off.

"Who are the Bickersons?" asked Annie.

Selina sighed. "Lord and Lady Bickerson are aristocrats from London," she said. "They're friends of Florence's family. Come and meet them, brave American children. It might be good for your education."

The boat rocked gently on the calm water as Jack and Annie followed Selina across the deck. "Aristocrats?" Annie whispered to Jack. "That's like royalty, right?"

"Sort of," said Jack. "We have to act proper."

"No problem," said Annie. "We've hung out with Empress Maria Theresa of Austria and King Philip the Second of Macedonia."

"Yeah, well, don't mention that to anyone," said Jack.

"Duh," said Annie.

Selina stopped in front of one of the cabin doors and took a deep breath. "Are you ready?" she asked Jack and Annie.

"Yes!" said Jack, eager to get out of the heat and away from the flies.

Selina opened the door and motioned for Jack and Annie to follow her. They walked into a small sitting room with green paneled walls and dark woodwork.

It took a moment for Jack's eyes to adjust to the shadowy room. It was much cooler inside than outside, but the red-faced man and woman sitting stiffly on straight-backed chairs were both fanning themselves frantically.

"Lord and Lady Bickerson, hello! I am sorry that Florence is not here now. I'm sure she will be back soon!" said Selina. "But in the meantime, please meet Jack and Annie from America."

"Hello," Jack said with a bow.

"Greetings, my lord. Greetings, my lady," Annie said with a curtsy.

The aristocrats barely nodded. They fanned themselves harder.

"Have a seat, children," said Selina.

Jack and Annie sat on the edge of the sofa. Jack tried to keep his back as straight as he could. When he saw Lady Bickerson scowl at his hat, he quickly pulled it off.

"How are your lordship and ladyship today?" asked Selina.

The two aristocrats spoke at once. "Terrible and wretched!" said Lord Bickerson. "Burning up!" said his wife.

"Oh, I'm so sorry," said Selina. But Jack noticed she didn't sound sorry at all.

"We saw a dreadful beast this morning!" said Lady Bickerson.

"A dreadful beast?" Selina repeated.

"Yes, a crocodile!" said Lord Bickerson. "And a servant told us a hippopotamus was spotted upriver yesterday. Nile hippos kill people, you know.

And Egyptian jackals have been seen recently, too. They come out at night and slay small animals." He looked at Jack and Annie. "They have even been known to attack children."

"Furthermore, our servants have been telling us about the snakes in Egypt," said Lady Bickerson. "The black mamba, for instance. One bite from that monster contains enough poison to kill twenty people!"

"Oh, my, let's hope—" began Selina.

"Of course the biggest killer in this land is the vicious little mosquito!" Lord Bickerson interrupted. "Egyptian mosquitoes can carry terrible diseases. Malaria, for one . . . fever, coma, death!"

"Oh, such misery," said Selina.

"Yes, aren't we *all* terribly miserable and frightened in Thebes?" said Lady Bickerson.

"Actually I'm not miserable *or* frightened," Annie said thoughtfully. "We saw a crocodile today, too. But it was harmless." She smiled at Lord and Lady Bickerson. They stared back at Annie as if *she* were a little mosquito.

Suddenly a servant threw open the door, stood at attention, and spoke in a loud voice. "Countess von Kensky!"

A glamorous-looking woman draped in a red silk shawl bustled in. Her dark hair was piled high on her head. On her shoulder was a tiny monkey. The monkey looked like a little elf, with a wrinkled face, big, pointed ears, and bushy eyebrows.

"Ohhh, look! It's so cute!" cried Annie.

"Countess von Kensky, I believe you have met Lord and Lady Bickerson?" said Selina.

"Oh, yes!" said the countess, nodding to the Bickersons. "But neither Koku nor I have met these lovely children! Who are you?"

"Jack and Annie from America," said Annie.

"Delightful!" said the countess. "Jack and Annie, this is Koku von Kensky! I am from Budapest, Hungary, but she is a baby baboon from the Sudan, in Africa! Koku, say hello." As the countess leaned down toward Jack and Annie, Koku grabbed Jack's ear with her tiny fingers and yanked hard.

"Oww!" Jack said.

The baby baboon grinned as if she thought Jack was funny. "Koku! No! No!" said the countess, pulling Koku's hand from Jack's ear.

A big *no-no,* thought Jack, rubbing his ear.

Uhh-woh, said the baboon, looking at Jack with her big eyes.

"*Uhh-woh* yourself!" said Annie, laughing and reaching out to pet Koku.

"Careful, child! She'll bite you!" said Lord Bickerson.

"Excuse me, my lord, but my darling Koku *never* bites," said the countess.

The look on the Bickersons' faces grew even more sour as Annie rubbed the baboon's spiky-haired little head.

Koku stared at Annie with bright, curious eyes, then let out a shrill screech. Annie screeched back at her. Everyone laughed, except, of course, the aristocrats, who now glared at Annie and Koku as if they were *both* little mosquitoes.

Before the Bickersons could speak, the door

opened again. A tall, slender woman stepped inside. Clutching a notebook, she was breathless, sunburned, and smiling. But her smile quickly

turned to a look of dismay when she saw all the visitors.

"Florence! Finally!" exclaimed Selina.

Florence Nightingale wore a plain gray dress. Her brown hair was parted in the middle.

"Hello, Florence, my dear," Lord Bickerson said. "Please sit down."

Florence took a seat, then smiled politely. "Greetings, my lord, my lady," she said. Her eyes softened as they rested on the countess and the baby baboon. "Hello, Countess. How is our little Koku today?"

"Very happy!" said the countess. "She has just made two wonderful new friends from America!" She nodded toward Jack and Annie.

"Oh . . . hello . . . ?" said Florence.

"Hello," said Jack.

Annie couldn't speak. She just stared at Florence with wide eyes and a big grin.

"Flo, this is Jack and Annie," said Selina. "They want to meet you."

Florence looked puzzled. "But why?" she said.

"For some reason, they believe you are a world-famous nurse who works in hospitals," said Selina.

Florence looked curiously at Jack and Annie. "A world-famous nurse?" she said. "How strange."

"Strange, indeed," said Lady Bickerson with a snort. "Work in a hospital? It's unthinkable."

"Unthinkable, my lady?" said Florence.

"Well, your mother and father would certainly find it so," Lord Bickerson said huffily.

A sad expression crossed Florence's face as she looked back at Jack and Annie. "No, children," she said, "I am not a world-famous nurse. In fact, I have never, not even for one day, worked in a hospital. My family would find it *unthinkable*."

Selina jumped in to change the subject. "What Flo really loves is taking notes about the Egyptian ruins," she said to Jack and Annie. "That's why we make such wonderful traveling companions. She loves to take notes, and I love to sketch. Tell our guests about your morning, Flo."

"I was at the Temple of Luxor," said Florence, brightening. "I studied the paintings, particularly the ones of Anubis."

"Anubis?" said Jack.

"The jackal god," said Florence. "He is on many tomb walls. Ancient Egyptians believed jackals protected the dead. I find that so fascinating."

"That *is* fascinating," said Annie.

Lady Bickerson shuddered. "Ugh, I find it gruesome," she said.

"It's not gruesome at all, my lady," said Florence. "I find Egyptian mythology to be quite beautiful."

"I think so, too!" said Jack.

"Beautiful?" said Lord Bickerson. "I don't see how one could find anything in this land beautiful, Florence. I cannot imagine why you would want to prowl among those ghastly ruins."

"Nor I!" said Lady Bickerson. "They all stink of rats and decay."

"Oh! Speaking of rats," said the countess, "Koku and I saw one in our cabin last night. Neither of us could sleep a wink after that!"

"We *never* sleep!" said Lady Bickerson. "Not with the rats and flies and fleas! And that dreadful singing from our crew hurts my ears!"

"I'm sorry you find everything so distasteful in this land, my lady," said Florence. "It makes me wonder why you and your lordship ever chose to travel to Egypt in the first place."

"Why, these days, it's considered quite fashionable to visit Egypt," said Lady Bickerson. "Though now Lord Bickerson and I can't possibly understand why."

"I adore Egypt," Florence said. "And I feel I must defend her. Egypt and I quite agree with each other."

"Indeed?" said Lord Bickerson. "You adore Egypt, she agrees with you, and you feel you must defend her? You certainly seem to have an excellent opinion of yourself, Miss Nightingale."

Florence took a deep breath. Then she said quietly, "No, in truth, I do not have an excellent opinion of myself, my lord."

"*I* have an excellent opinion of you," Annie whispered.

An awkward silence filled the room.

"Forgive me," said Florence. "I am not feeling well. I must retire to my own cabin . . . I fear I must." And with that, Florence Nightingale rose from her chair and slipped soundlessly out of the room.

CHAPTER FOUR

Baboon Babysitters

Everyone was silent for a moment after Florence left. The Bickersons were the first to speak.

"Well!" said Lady Bickerson.

"How utterly rude!" said Lord Bickerson.

"Excuse me for a moment while I check on Flo," said Selina, a worried look on her face. "Perhaps the heat was too much for her today." And with that, Selina left the sitting room, too.

"Well!" said Lady Bickerson again.

"I hope I did not offend Miss Nightingale by complaining about the rat," said the countess.

"I like her very much. Miss Nightingale, I mean, not the rat."

"You do not know Florence as we do," said Lord Bickerson. "You have no idea of the trouble she has caused her family."

"It's shocking," said Lady Bickerson. "She refuses to behave like a lady. She is full of her own thoughts and opinions. She tells her poor mother she has dreams to leave home so she can work!"

"What's wrong with that?" asked Annie.

Uh-oh, thought Jack. Annie sounded angry.

"No proper lady works out in the world!" Lord Bickerson snapped.

"Why not?" asked Annie. "I mean, if you wanted to follow your dreams and people wouldn't let you, wouldn't you feel bad, too? And what's wrong with having thoughts and opinions? I have thoughts and opinions all the time!"

"What a rude child you are!" said Lady Bickerson. "Is that how your parents taught you to speak to your superiors?"

Jack was starting to get angry, too. "We don't

have superiors at home," he said.

Lord Bickerson glared at Jack and Annie. "It is high time you children left this boat," he said. "Miss Nightingale does not even know who you are. None of us know who you are, or who your parents are!"

"Excuse me, sir, but this is not your boat, is it?" Annie said. "I thought it belonged to Selina and Charles."

"Oooh!" the aristocrats both gasped.

Lord Bickerson strode to the door. "Be gone!" he said. "You children are the very definition of the word *impolite.* Leave before I send for the local governor! He'd know what to do with you!"

"Seriously? What does that mean?" said Jack.

"It means *go,*" said Annie, "which I'm happy to do."

"Me too," said Jack.

Jack and Annie stood up. As they headed for the door, Annie looked back at the countess and her baby baboon. "Good-bye, Countess. Good-bye, Koku. It was great meeting you."

Jack nodded in agreement.

"Must you leave?" said the countess.

"I fear we must," said Annie, echoing Florence. She curtsied, and Jack bowed. Then they both headed out the door.

Outside, the sun was brighter and hotter than ever. Flies buzzed everywhere. Jack put his hat back on. "Come on, let's get away from these beasts," he said.

"The flies or the aristocrats?" asked Annie.

"Both!" said Jack.

Jack and Annie headed over the gangplank to the riverbank, then walked toward some shade trees at the edge of the Nile. "Send for the local governor? *Seriously?*" said Jack.

"*Their* behavior was unthinkable!" said Annie. "The very definition of *impolite!*"

Jack laughed, but then he sighed. "We blew it," he said. "We got sidetracked. How can we complete our mission now?"

"Don't worry, we'll wait for the Bickersons to leave," said Annie. "Then we'll try to get back on board and visit with Florence."

"Okay, sounds like a plan. Sort of," said Jack.

"C'mon. Let's wait on that big rock under the trees," said Annie.

Jack and Annie headed toward the shady rock. Not far away, Mustafa was sitting next to his rowboat, reading a book. The guide looked up, gave them a nod, then went back to his reading. Across the river, Ali was resting with his donkeys.

"Could you believe the way those two talked about Florence?" said Annie. "She can't be a nurse. She can't work outside her house. She can't even have her own opinions! How do you become great if people make you feel so bad about yourself? And did you notice how they tried to make us afraid of everything? That was crazy."

"Yeah ... crazy," said Jack. But the aristocrats' warnings *had* gotten to him. Now he was on alert for all the beasts of the Nile. *What do black mambas look like?* he wondered. *Do jackals ever come out during the day?* When he heard the whine of a mosquito, he shook his head as if his hair were on fire.

"What's wrong with you?" said Annie.

Before Jack could answer, he heard a loud call.
WAHOO!

Jack and Annie jumped up and whirled around.

"Koku!" cried Annie.

The baby baboon was scrambling toward them on all fours. Countess von Kensky hurried after her. "Koku! Wait!" she called.

Koku leapt into Annie's arms. "Well, hello!" cried Annie, hugging the baby baboon.

"She wanted to find you!" the countess said, out of breath. "After you left, she screeched at the Bickersons. She even shook her little fists. So they ordered her off the boat, too! Now the poor couple is sitting there all alone!"

"Oh, thank you, Koku, for sticking up for us!" said Annie.

"I can see you like Koku and that she likes you," said the countess. "Therefore I have a favor to ask you. Could you care for her this afternoon? I must take a ferry downriver to see a sick friend, but I cannot take Koku. My friend is afraid of creatures from the wild."

"Of course we'll take care of her!" said Annie.

"Uh, Annie? You know we have a mission, right?" Jack said under his breath. Their job was to find a secret of greatness—not to babysit a baboon.

"Don't worry, Koku won't get in the way," Annie said to Jack. She looked at the countess. "We'd love to!"

"Thank you! Thank you very much! I trust you to be wonderful caretakers!" said the countess. She reached into her purse, brought out a chunk of brown bread, and gave it to Jack. "Please give her bits of this when she is hungry or sad. I won't be back until nightfall. Where can we rendezvous then?"

"Rendezvous?" said Annie.

"Yes, meet up with each other," said the countess.

"Oh—how about Selina's boat?" said Jack.

"Good, good! You two are angels who dropped from heaven! Thank you so very much!" said the countess. "Be good, Koku!" And she hurried down the riverbank to catch her ferry.

Uhh-woh? said Koku, looking after the countess.

"Don't be sad, baby," said Annie, sitting back on the rock. "Your mom won't be gone long."

Uhh-woh, the baboon said. She settled into Annie's lap, and Annie kissed her head.

"Would Koku like a snack?" Jack asked. He

broke off a piece of bread and gave it to her. He put the rest in his pouch.

Koku held the bread with her two tiny hands. She chewed thoughtfully, looking from Jack to Annie with her bright eyes. She uttered funny little noises between bites. Suddenly she screeched and pointed upriver.

Jack and Annie turned to look. Florence had left Charles and Selina's boat! Carrying a small bag, she was walking quickly down the riverbank toward Mustafa.

"Now's our chance!" Jack said.

"Let's go!" said Annie. Holding Koku, she hurried with Jack to Florence and the guide.

"I'd like to explore the Valley of the Queens," Florence was saying to Mustafa as Jack and Annie approached.

"Hi there!" said Annie.

Florence turned around. She looked startled. "Oh. Hello," she said.

Koku let out another screech.

"We're babysitting Koku," Annie explained.

Florence nodded. Jack could tell she didn't really want to talk to them.

"Are you going to take more notes this afternoon?" Annie asked.

"Yes . . . I am," Florence answered.

"You're just like Jack," said Annie. "He loves to write in his notebook, too."

"Oh. How nice," said Florence. Jack was embarrassed. Florence's mind was clearly on other things. She nodded politely, and then turned back to the guide. "Shall we be off, Mustafa?"

Mustafa helped Florence into the rowboat and took his position. As the guide picked up his oars, Florence glanced back at Jack, Annie, and Koku. They were all just standing on the bank, staring at her.

Florence sighed. "Do you need a ride to the western shore?" she said.

"Yes, please," said Annie.

"Then come," Florence said. "You are welcome to join us."

"Thanks!" said Annie.

Jack didn't say anything. He didn't feel welcome at all.

Jack and Annie climbed in with Koku and sat behind Florence. Mustafa used his oars to push the boat off the riverbank. As he began rowing across the Nile, the white-bearded guide sang the same peaceful song he'd sung before.

Annie gave Jack a thumbs-up sign.

Not really, Jack thought. Florence was sitting with her back to them now, writing in her notebook. How could they ever get her to pay attention to them?

"Look up *Valley of the Queens,*" Annie whispered to him. Jack took the handbook out of the pouch on his belt. Then he and Annie silently read:

About 3,000 years ago, the wives of the pharaohs were buried in the Valley of the Queens, near the Valley of the Kings. The tombs were cut out of limestone cliffs.

"Excuse me, Miss Nightingale?" Annie said.

"Have you ever been to the Valley of the Queens?"

Without looking back, Florence shook her head.

"We find it fascinating," said Annie. She nudged Jack, letting him know it was his turn to speak.

"Did you know that the wives of the pharaohs were buried there about three thousand years ago?" Jack said. "I believe their tombs were cut out of the limestone cliffs."

Florence barely nodded. She didn't say a word or look back at them. Before Jack or Annie could think of another way to get her attention, the rowboat arrived on the western shore.

CHAPTER FIVE

Valley of the Queens

"Miss Nightingale, your donkey!" Ali called out. The small boy stood with a donkey and a larger packhorse.

"How lovely to see you, Ali," said Florence.

Mustafa stepped into the shallow water and pulled the rowboat onto the bank. He then helped everyone out of the boat.

Jack and Annie stood with Koku and watched Florence mount the donkey. Mustafa climbed onto his packhorse. Jack felt helpless. He didn't know how to stop Florence from leaving them.

"Have a nice afternoon," said Annie.

Florence looked back at them. "I hope you have a nice afternoon, too," she said. "I would ask you to join me, but I am . . . well, I'm afraid I need a bit of quiet and solitude right now."

"We understand," said Annie.

"Thank you," said Florence. She turned back to the guide. "Lead the way, Mustafa."

Mustafa and his horse headed away from the river. Florence followed on her donkey. Jack, Annie, and Koku watched as they headed up the dirt road toward the distant mountains. Soon they disappeared from view.

"Darn," breathed Annie.

"Yeah," said Jack.

"Donkeys for you, too?" Ali asked, coming up behind them. "You can travel to the ruins without a guide, you know."

Annie looked at Jack. "Want to?" she asked.

"How do we get to the Valley of the Queens?" Jack asked Ali.

"Very easy." The boy pointed to the road.

"Travel the same way they went," he said. "Follow that road and never turn."

"That sounds simple," said Annie. "Let's go."

"Wait," said Jack. He took all of his Egyptian coins from his pouch and showed them to Ali. "Do we have enough to rent two donkeys?"

"Oh, yes!" Ali took only one coin. "Good for two donkeys all afternoon," he said.

"Okay, we'll do it," said Jack.

"Yay!" said Annie.

"Good. I will get them for you," said Ali. He headed to the donkeys standing under the trees.

"I wonder if there's anything we need to know about riding donkeys," said Jack. He opened their travelers' handbook again and looked up *donkey.* He read aloud:

Donkeys were first trained to carry travelers over 6,000 years ago in Egypt. The animals are easy to ride. But the traveler must approach them slowly and treat them with kindness and affection.

"Easy!" said Annie. "That's the way I always treat animals."

HEE-HAW!

"Here they are!" said Ali, leading two donkeys toward Jack and Annie.

Both donkeys were sandy brown with sweet faces. Their saddles were blankets made of heavy cloth. Their long, furry ears twitched to keep the flies away.

"Hello there!" Annie said to one of the donkeys. "You have ears like a rabbit. Can I call you Bunny?"

"Oh, brother," said Jack.

"Talk to yours, too," Annie coached Jack. "Call her a sweet name. Kindness and affection, remember?"

Jack rolled his eyes and scratched the ears of the other donkey. "Hi ... um ... Honey. Want to go for a ride?" he said. The donkey nuzzled her head against Jack's hand.

Ali laughed. "I think my donkeys like you very much," he said.

Holding Koku, Annie climbed onto the back of Bunny, while Jack climbed onto Honey.

"You must take water," said Ali. He tied tin canteens to the donkeys' saddles. "Come back by sundown. There is danger in the hills after dark."

"Like what kind of danger?" asked Jack.

"Wild jackals, tomb raiders," said Ali.

"Got it," said Jack.

"We'll be back before dark," said Annie.

"*Way* before dark," said Jack.

"Good-bye, Ali. Thank you!" said Annie. "Giddy-up, Bunny!" She led the way with Koku on her shoulder.

"Follow them, Honey, please," said Jack.

The two donkeys left the lush riverbank and trotted up the same road that Mustafa and Florence had traveled.

"Our donkeys remind me of the camels we rode to Baghdad!" Annie called back to Jack. "Remember Beauty and Cutie?"

"Oh, brother," said Jack. The camels had nearly ruined their mission.

Bunny and Honey trotted past cornfields, palm trees, sheep, goats, mud huts, and children playing in the dirt. When the children saw Jack and Annie, they laughed and pointed at the baboon riding on Annie's shoulder.

Soon the dirt road opened onto a wider, rougher road that crossed a flat plain. The plain was bordered by the sand-colored mountains. Hot breezes blew clouds of dust as the donkeys clomped side by side over the dry, cracked earth.

Through the gritty haze, Jack could see ruins scattered about the plain—broken columns and chunks of ancient walls half buried in sand.

"Look!" said Annie.

Two gigantic statues loomed ahead against the blue sky: enormous pharaohs on thrones, as tall as five-story buildings.

"Let's stop for a minute," Jack called. He pulled on his donkey's reins and took out the travelers' handbook. He found a picture of the statues and read aloud:

> **More than 3,000 years old, the Colossi of Memnon once guarded the temple of a pharaoh.** *Memnon* **means** *Ruler of the Dawn.* **Ancient Egyptians believed one of the giant statues sang every day at sunrise.**

Jack took out his notebook and pencil and wrote:

Memnon=Ruler of the Dawn

He looked at the ruins again. The pharaoh's temple had vanished with time. The statues were faceless, their bodies broken and worn away by thousands of years of wind and sand. The wounded giants still looked amazingly powerful, though. Through the dry heat, Jack could imagine their ancient song.

HEE-HAW!

Jack jumped. "What's that?"

"A donkey! Up ahead somewhere," said Annie, "past those temple ruins. I'll bet it's Florence's donkey. Hurry! Let's go!"

Jack put away his notebook and pencil and the handbook. "Giddyup!" he said, and his donkey started walking again. "Annie, when we find Florence, try to act surprised, so she won't think we're following her. Be cool."

"Don't worry, I'm always cool," said Annie. "But we'll have to find a way to stick close to her, so we can find out her secret of greatness."

"Yeah," Jack sighed. "The only problem is I'm having trouble seeing what makes her so great," he said. He thought Florence seemed unhappy and unfriendly.

"But she *is* great," said Annie. "I know she is!"

Jack and Annie kept riding their donkeys

through the heat and dust. When they stopped at the ruins of an ancient temple, there were no signs of Florence or Mustafa among the broken columns and crumbling walls. There were no signs of any living things.

"I don't see them," said Jack. "We must have lost them somewhere." He shivered, despite the heat. The quiet felt spooky to him. He grabbed his canteen and took a long drink of water. Annie did the same. Then she poured a little bit of water into her cupped hand and offered it to Koku.

"Do you think we should keep going to the Valley of the Queens?" asked Annie.

"I guess so," said Jack.

"Florence and Mustafa are probably already there," said Annie. "Giddyup, Bunny."

As the donkeys walked toward the cliffs, Jack couldn't shake his uneasy feeling. Everything was the color of mud and sand. The only other living creatures were some vultures circling in the sky. As Jack stared up at the birds, Annie brought her donkey to a halt.

"Oh, wow! Those must be the tombs of the pharaohs' wives!" said Annie. She pointed to several huge square holes carved into the limestone walls of the cliffs.

"Yeah." Jack shuddered. "You know, I think I'd like to go back. This place gives me the creeps."

"Are you afraid of ghosts?" said Annie.

Jack shook his head. "I don't know. Maybe. Let's just go," he said. "We can wait for Florence back at Charles and Selina's boat."

"Don't you at least want to peek inside one of the tombs?" asked Annie.

"Nope," Jack said.

"Well, okay, you don't have to," said Annie. "But if I don't take a look, I'll always wonder what I missed. Koku and I will be right back."

"No, Annie, let's leave this place," said Jack.

"Just one teeny minute," said Annie. Holding on to the baby baboon, she climbed off her donkey. "We'll just take a quick look in that one." She pointed to the nearest tomb cut into the mountain. "I promise we won't go inside. We'll hurry back."

With Koku sitting on her shoulder, Annie took off toward the tomb.

Jack's donkey shook her head and kicked her hind legs. "What's wrong, Honey?" said Jack.

Annie's donkey started acting strangely, too. She brayed loudly and turned away from the cliffs. "Calm down, Bunny," said Jack, trying to speak in a soothing voice. "It's okay, it's okay."

Something was clearly bothering both animals. Jack's donkey tried to turn around, and Annie's donkey began trotting back the way they'd come!

"Wait, Bunny!" Jack called as Annie's donkey sped away. "Annie!" he shouted. "Come back *now*! Bunny's running off!"

Annie was standing at the entrance of the tomb. She turned around. "What?" she called.

Koku let out a bone-chilling shriek. From behind a pile of rocks near the tomb came two dirty, gray, wolf-like animals. The two creatures looked at Annie, then loped in her direction.

"Oh, man!" said Jack. *"Jackals!"*

CHAPTER SIX

No Big Deal

Annie turned and saw the jackals running toward her. "Oh, no!" she cried.

Shrieking, Koku leapt from Annie's arms and bounded across the dry, cracked ground. When the jackals saw the baby baboon, they stopped. Then, cackling and yelping, they took off after her.

Koku screeched and bolted toward the mountain. The jackals were right behind her.

"NOOO!" screamed Annie. She tore after Koku and the jackals.

"Annie!" Jack yelled. He jumped off his donkey and ran after her.

From a distance, Jack saw the baby baboon disappear into a crack between two cliffs. Howling and cackling, the jackals followed Koku. They slipped into the crack and vanished from sight.

Annie was racing to catch up. Jack was far behind. When he finally reached her, Annie was desperately trying to squeeze through the narrow opening.

"We can't fit through there!" said Jack.

"We have to save Koku!" Annie cried.

They heard shrieking, yelping, and cackling above them. Then gradually the sounds faded away.

"KOKU!" screamed Annie.

Dead silence.

"Oh, no! I think they got her!" Annie wailed. "I think they got her, Jack!" She burst into tears. "Koku, Koku," she repeated, sobbing.

Jack didn't know what to say. Everything had happened so fast! Then suddenly he heard another sound.

WAHOO!

"Annie!" Jack grabbed her by the shoulders and shook her. "Listen!"

Annie put her hand over her mouth. Tears rolled down her cheeks as she listened.

WAHOO! The sound came from high above them.

Jack and Annie stepped back and looked up the steep cliff. Koku was at the very top, jumping up and down, screeching at them.

"She made it!" cried Annie. "She got away! Koku, come down! Come down!"

"Where're the jackals?" said Jack.

"I'll bet it's too steep for them to climb up after her!" said Annie. "Koku, come down!"

The baby baboon paced back and forth along the edge of the cliff, crying.

"We have to go get her!" said Annie. "She's afraid to come down."

Koku screeched and waved her arms.

"We can't climb up there," said Jack. "It's too steep."

"We have to try!" said Annie.

"We're not rock climbers," said Jack, looking up at the steep wall of limestone. "Only the best rock climbers in the world could get up there."

"We can do that!" said Annie. "We can be great rock climbers."

"You can't just *be* one," said Jack. "You have to

go through lots of training and practice—"

"The mist!" Annie said. "We can use the magic mist and make a wish to be great rock climbers!"

"Use the mist?" said Jack. They could only use the mist once, and it was supposed to help them with their mission. But when he looked up at the baby baboon crying and waving her arms, saving Koku seemed more important than anything.

"Okay!" said Jack. "We'll use the mist to get her down. But we might have to walk back. I'll bet both our donkeys have run far away by now."

"No problem! We can do that!" said Annie. "Hurry! Before the jackals come back!"

Jack reached into his leather pouch and pulled out the tiny bottle. He uncorked the top.

"Here goes!" Jack said. "I wish to be a great rock climber!" He slowly inhaled the magic mist. His nostrils filled with the scent of mountain air and cold, moving water. The fresh, clean smell filled him with strength and energy.

Jack handed the bottle to Annie. "I wish to be a great rock climber!" she exclaimed. Annie inhaled the mist, too. Then she gave the bottle back to Jack. He corked it and put it away.

Jack and Annie looked up at the steep wall of the limestone cliff.

"No big deal," said Jack.

"Easy," said Annie. She called up to the baby baboon, "We're coming, Koku. Don't worry. We'll save you!"

"We have one hour to climb up and back down," said Jack. "First we need to take off our boots, so our toes can fit in the cracks."

"Righto," said Annie. She and Jack coolly slipped off their boots and stockings.

"Okay. Now we follow the three basic rules of rock climbing," said Jack. "We look. We think. We move."

"Got it," said Annie.

Jack and Annie moved about twenty feet apart. They each studied the cliff wall as if it were a giant map.

Jack looked for cracks, ledges, bumps, and holes. After he'd charted his route in his mind, he took a long, deep breath. He lodged the toes of his left foot into a crack in the limestone. He reached high and gripped two tiny bumps on the wall with his fingers. Then he pulled himself up. Out of the corner of his eye, he saw Annie doing the same thing.

Jack and Annie climbed higher and higher up the wall. Jack took his time to find new cracks for his toes. He slowly ran his hands over the rock face to find bumps and ledges to grab with his fingers.

As an expert rock climber, Jack knew exactly how to shift his body weight and when to relax his grip. He knew exactly how to push with his legs and when to pull with his hands.

Annie was silently climbing up the cliff at the same time, but Jack didn't look at her or think of her. He completely ignored Koku's screeching from above. He kept all his attention focused on finding new places to grip the face of the cliff with his fingers and toes.

Slowly and calmly, Jack gripped, pulled, and pushed his way up the face of the cliff. He climbed and climbed until he was only a few feet from the top. He couldn't see over the ledge, but he gripped tightly with his fingertips and hoisted himself higher.

WAHOO!

Koku poked her head over the edge of the cliff, breaking Jack's concentration. She reached down and grabbed his ear.

"Oww!" Jack yelled. His left hand lost its grip. His right foot slipped. Then his left foot slipped! Jack was hanging on to the ledge with just one hand—and that hand was slipping! "Annieee!" he yelled.

Just as Jack was about to lose his grip and fall, he felt a hand clamp down on his right wrist.

"Hold on!" Annie cried. She'd reached the top ahead of him! Jack's fingers slipped from the ledge, but Annie held on to his wrist with both hands as he dangled high above the stony ground below.

The baby baboon shrieked. The vultures cawed in the cloudless sky.

"You're still a great rock climber, Jack!" Annie shouted. "You know how to do this!"

I know how to do this! Jack thought. He clicked back into thinking like an expert rock climber. He twisted himself toward the rock wall. He reached out with his free hand and secured his fingertips in a small crevice. He planted his bare toes onto two ridges.

"Okay! I'm good," called Jack. "You can let go."

Annie released Jack's hand. He quickly gripped a small bump on the rock face. He was very still for a moment. Blocking out all sounds and thoughts, he waited for his breathing to slow down. He waited for his legs to stop shaking and for his body to relax.

Using all his strength, Jack pulled himself upward. He lifted his leg over the rim of the limestone cliff. Then he gracefully pulled his whole body up and over the edge.

"Whew," breathed Jack. He was safe.

CHAPTER SEVEN

Panic

*W*AHOO!

Koku shrieked and jumped up and down.

Annie slapped Jack on the back. "You did it!" she cried.

"*We* did it," Jack said, breathing hard. "Thanks for saving me when I lost my grip!" He shook his finger at the baby baboon. "Bad time for an ear grab, Koku von Kensky!"

Koku pressed her lips against Jack's cheek and gave him a kiss. "Eww, gross!" said Jack, laughing.

"She's so happy we saved her!" said Annie.

Jack glanced down at the ground below the cliffs to make sure the jackals hadn't returned. "Okay, let's rest a minute," he said. He sat back, closed his eyes, and took a long, deep breath.

"Koku, would you like a treat?" Annie said.

"Here," said Jack. He opened his eyes and reached into his pouch. He took out a bit of bread and gave it to Koku. She chewed happily as the three of them sat together, looking out over the land of western Thebes.

"What a great view," said Jack.

The sun was setting behind the honey-colored mountains, and the River Nile glimmered with golden light. The cornfields were golden, too, as herds of sheep and goats headed home. Jack felt the same calm feeling he'd felt during his climb. He felt free of all his fears and worries.

As the sky turned from gold to red to dark purple, the wind began to blow. The air grew cooler. Sand swirled around the two Colossi of Memnon. Jack imagined that the giants' breath was stirring

the sands. He shivered and pulled out the handbook and looked at the map of Thebes.

"Okay. On the other side of the Nile are the
Temples of Karnak and Luxor," Jack said. He
looked across the Nile to the distant temples. Beyond the temples, a full moon was starting to rise.
Jack looked back at the map. "And on this side of
the Nile are the Valley of the Kings and the Valley
of the Queens."

"Look!" said Annie. She pointed to the fallen
temple near the road to the river. "Do you see two
people?"

Sure enough, in the distance two people were
riding a horse and a donkey. "It's them!" Jack said.
"Florence and Mustafa! Maybe they can help us
get back, since we don't have donkeys anymore."
He stood up and waved his arms. "Hello!"

Annie joined him. "Hello!" she yelled. But Florence and Mustafa didn't seem to hear them as they
rode back toward the Nile.

"Hello!" Annie called once more, but it was
no use.

"Well, we'll just walk fast and catch up with them at the boat," said Jack.

"We still have time to get down, don't we?" said Annie. "I mean, our hour isn't up yet, is it?"

"I . . . I don't think so," said Jack. He couldn't believe he'd forgotten about the time! "How long did it take us to climb up? How long have we been sitting here?"

"I don't know," said Annie.

The sun had sunk below the horizon, and the sky was quickly growing dark.

"We have to hurry!" said Jack. "Before our hour runs out! Before we lose our rock-climbing skills! Before it gets darker! Before the hills become more dangerous!"

"Relax, Jack," said Annie. "Remember, rock climbers go slowly. We look. We think. We move."

"Right," said Jack. "Right. Okay." He took a deep breath and tried to slow his racing heart. He tried not to think about running out of time, or losing their rock-climbing skills, or the danger in the dark valley.

"You okay?" said Annie.

"Yes," said Jack.

They looked over the edge of the cliff at the rock face. Jack realized he still knew exactly what to do. "No big deal," he said.

"No big deal," echoed Annie.

Jack mapped out his route to the ground. He located bumps . . . ledges . . . holes . . . ridges . . . cracks . . . until he had a good plan.

"I'll carry Koku on my back. She's not heavy," said Annie. "I'll start down over there." She moved about twenty feet away from Jack. "Don't forget, go slowly," she reminded Jack. "And don't freak out! We look, we think, we move."

"Yeah, right, I know," said Jack. "Just concentrate on yourself."

Jack turned away from Annie and Koku. He took a full, deep breath. When he felt a perfect balance between calm and alertness, he started down the cliff wall.

Jack inched smoothly along the face of the

rock, shifting his weight and keeping his eyes on his feet. He reached down to lower ledges with his toes and lodged his fingertips in the cracks above. He kept his body straight and didn't lean too closely into the rock. Jack knew exactly what to do—until he was halfway down. Then suddenly he didn't know *anything*.

Jack froze. His body started to shake. His toes slipped from the cracks they were in. His hands slipped from the ridge he was gripping. He fell.

Jack hit the ground so hard he couldn't breathe. His whole body screamed with pain, especially his right shoulder and arm.

"Jaaack!" Annie cried out from above him. Then there was a terrible thud.

Jack heard Koku shriek. He wanted desperately to help Annie and the baby baboon, but he was still struggling to breathe. He couldn't stand up. He couldn't move at all!

Jackals started howling. It sounded like many

more than just two. It sounded like a whole pack.
The howling grew louder, then faded away.

"An-An...," Jack whispered. He couldn't
even say her name. The wind made loud whistling
sounds through the limestone cliffs.

Jack was cold and scared. He worried that his
bones were broken. He worried that Annie was
hurt—or worse, maybe not alive.

Koku made whining, weepy sounds. Then Jack
heard a moan: *"Jack!"*

"Annie!" Jack said hoarsely. In spite of the
pain, he forced himself to sit up. He saw Annie on
the ground, lying not far from him.

"I got the breath—knocked—out of me," she
said, gasping. "Couldn't breathe. Or talk. Now my
ankle ... ohhh ...," she groaned.

"Hold on, don't move!" said Jack. As he strug-
gled to a standing position, he discovered that he
couldn't lift his right arm at all. It just hung limply
from his shoulder at a strange angle.

Jack took a deep breath. He clutched his bad
arm and walked barefoot to Annie. He had no idea

where they'd left their boots. It was too dark to find them now.

"Ohhh," said Annie. She was lying on her side, holding her right ankle and moaning.

"Can you stand up?" said Jack.

"Maybe," said Annie.

"I'll help," said Jack. He used one hand to help Annie roll onto her back and stand up.

"OWW!" she cried.

"Sorry, sorry," said Jack.

Annie tried to laugh. "No, *I'm* sorry," she said. "I didn't mean to yell, but it really hurts if I put weight on it. What can we do? How can we get back?"

"Don't worry, I can walk," said Jack. "You can lean on me and hop on one foot."

"Are you sure you're not too badly hurt?" asked Annie.

"No big deal," Jack said. "Just lean on my left side. We'll be fine."

"Okay." Annie placed her arm on Jack's shoulder.

"Here, Koku, hold my hand tight," said Annie.

She held out her left hand, and the baby baboon
grabbed it.

"Ready, everyone?" Jack asked.

"Ready," said Annie.

"Good," said Jack. "Let's give it a try."

CHAPTER EIGHT

Moon over the Nile

Jack took halting steps, supporting much of Annie's weight as she hopped on her left foot. His shoulder hurt terribly, but he tried to hide his pain from Annie. The Valley of the Queens felt spookier than ever. *The jackals must be close by,* Jack thought. And what about those tomb raiders that Ali had mentioned?

"Do we know the way back?" Annie asked.

"From the top of the cliff, we could see the moon rising over the Nile," said Jack. "So, if we walk toward the moon now, we should come to the river."

"Good thinking," said Annie.

Heading toward the moon and holding on to Annie, Jack kept walking slowly. "Oww!" Annie said softly with each hop she took.

Annie's hopping jostled Jack's body, sending pain through his shoulder and arm. But he gritted his teeth and tried not to make a sound. He was afraid Annie wouldn't let him help her if she found out how much he was hurting.

After only about fifty yards, Jack knew he couldn't support Annie's weight much longer. "Okay—let's stop for a minute and rest—" he said.

Koku screeched. She let go of Annie's hand and bounded away. "Koku!" cried Annie. "Come back!"

Oh, no, not again! thought Jack. *Did she hear jackals?*

"Look, there's a light!" said Annie. She pointed at a flickering light moving toward them.

"We have to be quiet," Jack whispered. "It could be tomb raiders."

"Tomb raiders?" said Annie, peering into the dark. "I don't think so." She called out, "We're here! We're over here! Help us!"

"Children?" a woman called.

"We're here!" Annie cried again.

Koku screeched and came running back toward Annie and Jack. She chattered and jumped up and down.

Out of the dark, Florence Nightingale appeared on her donkey. She was wearing a shawl and holding a lantern. Mustafa followed behind her on his packhorse.

"It's us, Jack and Annie!" cried Annie.

"Thank goodness!" said Florence. "We've been looking for you! When we arrived at the river, Ali reported that your donkeys had returned without you!"

"We were trying to save Koku from jackals," said Annie. "She escaped from them and then got stuck on top of a cliff. We got up there okay, but we fell coming down!"

"You poor things!" cried Florence, climbing off her donkey. "Please bring water for them, Mustafa!"

Mustafa dismounted and untied two canteens from his saddle. Florence carried her lamp over to Jack and Annie. "Are you hurt, my dears?" she asked in a soft, comforting voice.

"Yes, I hurt my ankle," said Annie. "But I think Jack's in worse shape, even though he says it's no big deal."

"It's just my shoulder and my arm," Jack said to Florence.

"Oh, my goodness, you are lucky—both of you—to be alive!" said Florence. She gently felt Jack's shoulder and arm. He winced with pain and groaned. "Can you move it, dear?" she asked him.

"No," he said.

Mustafa handed Jack a canteen and gave one to Annie, too. While Jack and Annie gulped down water, Florence spoke softly to Mustafa. "Let's take them straight to the boat," she said. "Jack can ride my donkey, and Annie and the little baboon can ride on your horse." Then she turned back to Jack and Annie. "Mustafa and I will walk alongside you."

"Thank you," said Jack. He was relieved to have someone else in charge.

Mustafa brought the packhorse over to them and carefully lifted Annie and Koku onto the saddle. Then he helped Jack climb onto the back of the donkey.

"Good. Now let us go," said Florence. She blew out the flame in her lamp. Mustafa tied it to the saddle of the packhorse, along with the canteens.

By the light of the moon, Mustafa led the animals through the chilly night. Florence walked beside the donkey, staying close to Jack.

They all traveled silently over the barren, stony ground until they came to the statues of the ancient pharaoh. The giants looked like faceless gray ghosts in the moonlight.

As the group headed down the dirt road toward the Nile, Jack did his best to sit up straight on the donkey's back. But every step the animal took brought Jack more pain. Once or twice he couldn't help crying out.

"Jack," Annie called to him in a soft voice.

"Remember what it felt like to be rock climbers?"

Though the words might have sounded strange to Mustafa and Florence, Jack knew exactly what Annie meant. "Yes," he breathed. He worked hard to remember what it had felt like to be a great rock climber, to feel calm and centered. He tried to block out the pain in his arm and shoulder by closing his eyes and concentrating on the sounds of the night.

Jack heard Koku making her baby baboon noises. He heard the cornstalks whispering in the wind. He heard the baaing of sheep and bleating of goats.

As they came closer to the Nile, he heard the rustling of reeds and croaking of frogs. He heard the *HEE-HAW* of donkeys.

Jack's eyes shot open. "Honey?" he said.

"Bunny?" Annie called out. "Is that you?"

"Hello! I have your two donkeys here!" Ali called, rushing toward the travelers. "They are safe! I am so glad that you are safe, too!"

"Can you please help us, Ali?" said Florence.

"We must get Jack and Annie back to the Brace-bridges' boat."

Ali quickly took the reins of the packhorse and donkey. Mustafa and Florence helped Jack, Annie, and Koku dismount. With Florence's help, Jack climbed into the rowboat. Mustafa picked up Annie and Koku and set them down next to Jack.

"Good night, Ali," said Florence as she and Mustafa finally climbed into the rowboat, too. "Your grandfather will be back soon to take you home."

"Good night, Miss Nightingale," said the small boy.

Mustafa's oars dipped into the water, and the boat started gliding across the river. As he rowed, the guide sang his rowing song in time to the splashing of the oars. The Nile waters sparkled, reflecting the moonlight. Jack loved the peaceful, mysterious feel of the ancient river.

When they reached the opposite shore, Mustafa tied up the rowboat at the water's edge. "Please help the children out of the boat," said

Florence. "Then you must hurry back to Ali. It is surely past his bedtime."

Mustafa nodded.

Florence turned to Jack and Annie. "I will be back in a moment with Charles and Selina," she said. She climbed out of the rowboat and hurried away.

Mustafa helped Jack, Annie, and Koku onto the grass. "Thank you," said Annie.

The old Egyptian nodded again. Then he got into his boat and began rowing across the glimmering Nile, heading back to his grandson.

"Are you okay?" Annie asked Jack.

"Fine," he breathed. He was in too much pain to say anything else.

Jack heard voices coming toward them. Florence was hurrying down the riverbank with Selina and Charles.

"Oh, my poor dears!" cried Selina. "And Koku! There *you* are!"

"Did the countess come looking for her?" said Annie.

"No, she sent word asking us to keep Koku for the night," said Selina.

"Oh, good. And—and can we stay, too?" Annie asked shyly. "We'll meet up with our parents tomorrow morning."

"Of course! Here, let me help you," said Charles, leaning down. "Put your arm around my shoulder."

Annie did as Charles said. He lifted her and carried her back toward the moored sailboat.

"We'll follow them, Jack," said Florence kindly. Florence and Selina walked on either side of Jack up the riverbank, and Koku clamored behind, shrieking and making noises. Jack imagined she was talking about their scary adventure in the dark hills.

Finally the group arrived at the large sailboat. "Home, sweet home!" said Selina.

"Into my cabin," said Florence.

Charles and Selina helped Jack and Annie into the middle door of the long cabin. Koku followed and leapt onto a tall bed.

Florence helped Jack take off his heavy longsleeved shirt, his belt, and his hat. "Now, make

room for the children, Koku," Florence said to the
baby baboon.

Jack and Annie climbed onto the large bed,
and Florence gently covered them with blan-

kets. "It gets quite cold at night," she explained
softly. She draped mosquito netting around the
bedposts as Selina lit kerosene lamps. Jack could
smell the kerosene as the flames flickered and

shadows danced on the green paneled walls.

The boat rocked on the Nile, and a soft breeze came through an open porthole. Through the gauze of the delicate mosquito netting, Florence, Charles, and Selina looked like dream figures—or angels—to Jack. He closed his eyes, and finally, he felt safe.

CHAPTER NINE

Heroes of the Dawn

Uhh-woh?

Jack felt Koku's little hand on his ear.

He opened his eyes. The mosquito netting had been pulled back. The baby baboon was perched on the headboard of the bed. She grabbed Jack's ear and tugged. He started to push her away, but to his surprise, his right arm was pinned across his chest. It was tucked tightly into a cotton sling.

"No, no, Koku!" said Annie. She pushed the baby baboon away from Jack. Florence Nightingale was sitting on the edge of the bed, wrapping a long piece of cloth around Annie's ankle.

"Hello, Jack!" said Florence with a lovely smile. "I hope you don't mind your sling. I maneuvered your arm into it while you were in a deep sleep."

"Thanks," he said.

"I'm afraid you dislocated your shoulder," said Florence. "It will be less painful if you wear the sling. As soon as you get to a city, you must see a doctor."

"I will, thanks," said Jack.

Florence finished pinning the cloth bandage snugly around Annie's ankle. "There, m'lady! Your ankle will heal as well. But you must go very slowly for a while," she said. She looked at Jack. "Your sister received a frightful sprain, but I'm happy to say she has broken no bones."

"Cool," said Jack.

Florence tucked Jack's blanket tighter around him. "There, soldier. Warmer now?"

Jack was confused at first; then he realized that Florence had thought he meant that he was cold when he said *cool.* He started to laugh, but it hurt his arm too much.

"Miss Nightingale, you really are a great nurse," said Annie. "What's your secret?"

"I have no secret," said Florence. "I have only taken care of friends and relatives. As you heard from Lord Bickerson, my family does not allow me to work. But I would *love* to be a nurse. That is my greatest dream in life. It is why I found it so strange that you two thought I *was* a nurse. And now, through entirely unpredictable circumstances, I have been a nurse to you both! Is that not a remarkable coincidence?" Florence shook her head with wonder. "Well. Please excuse me, and I will pour your tea." Florence stepped over to a small kerosene stove and poured water from a teakettle into two cups.

"Good try," Jack whispered to Annie. "She still doesn't have a clue that she's great. So how can she share her secret of greatness with us?"

"I don't know," said Annie. "This is tricky."

"Here you are," said Florence, returning with two cups of tea.

She handed Annie one cup, and then helped

Jack take the other in his left hand. Jack carefully brought it to his lips. The hot tea and honey tasted wonderful.

"So allow me to understand what you told me last night," said Florence. "You both risked your lives to save Koku?"

Jack and Annie nodded.

Florence smiled and turned to the baby baboon. "Little one, I believe your two friends are great heroes," she said.

"Not really," said Annie. "We're not like you. *You* are the great hero."

"What? How silly. Surely no one would call *me* a hero," said Florence.

"But they will," said Annie. "I know you're not a real nurse yet. But someday you're going to be the greatest nurse of all time."

Florence looked at Jack. "Did you actually see your sister fall from the cliff?" she said under her breath.

"No. Why?" Jack whispered.

"I worry she might have hit her head," said

Florence. "She does not seem in her right mind."

Jack laughed. "Don't worry, she's fine," he said. "What she says about you is true. We know it for a fact."

"Oh, dear, perhaps you *both* fell on your heads," said Florence. "I appreciate your gratitude, children, but an ankle bandage and a simple arm sling should not convince you I will be a great nurse."

"Well, what do *you* think makes a great nurse?" asked Annie.

"I—I have thought about that, actually," said Florence. "I would have to say: discipline . . . quickness . . . and kindness."

Annie slipped her hand out from under the blanket. She and Jack glanced at the Ring of Truth. It wasn't glowing.

"Good try," Jack whispered again.

"It seems like you definitely have those qualities," Annie said to Florence. "So why won't your family let you be a nurse?"

"They mean no harm," Florence said with a sigh. "They only want me to be a proper lady.

They will allow me to care for sick relatives and even some of the villagers. But they would never permit me to work in a hospital."

"That's so unfair!" said Annie. "The world needs you!"

"I don't believe the world needs me," Florence said, laughing. But then her expression grew more serious. "I *do* believe, though, that *I* need the world."

"What do you mean?" asked Jack.

"I just feel that I *must* do something good for the world, for the poor and the sick." Florence's voice became strong and passionate. "I must lift the load of pain from the suffering. I must do *more* than walk around the garden, write meaningless letters, sit in drawing rooms, gossip about the neighbors, arrange flowers, and go to dances! I must! One's work must be for the greater good of *all*, not just for oneself! I feel I must do something useful for the world, or I will go stark, raving mad." Florence's eyes shone.

Annie and Jack glanced down at the ring. It

wasn't glowing brightly yet, but it was glimmering a little.

"Uh . . . could you explain all that again in just a few simple words?" he said.

"Let's see . . . ," said Florence. "How to say it simply?" She stared out the window at the Nile. Then she spoke very clearly. "I truly believe, deep in my heart, that one's life must have *meaning* and *purpose*."

Jack and Annie looked at the Ring of Truth. It glimmered more and more . . . then glowed as brightly as a burning ember.

Koku shrieked and pointed at the ring. Annie and Jack both laughed. Annie quickly hid her hand under the blanket.

Florence turned back to them. "Did that sound funny?" she said. She seemed embarrassed.

"No, no!" said Annie. "It sounded . . ." She paused. "It sounded *true.*"

"Meaning and purpose," Jack repeated. "Do you think that's a secret of greatness?"

"Yes, I do," said Florence. "Do you agree?"

"Yes. Totally," said Jack.

"And we know you'll find a way to do it," said Annie. "Trust us."

A rooster crowed, then another, and another. The first light of dawn crept through the window.

"Listen to them all," said Florence. "It's a brand-new day."

"Yes!" agreed Annie.

The door to the cabin swung open. Countess von Kensky stood at the threshold, wrapped in her red shawl, her dark hair falling in curls around her shoulders. "Koku! My baby!" she cried.

The baboon screeched, bounded off the bed, and leapt into the countess's arms. The two of them waltzed around the room, the countess's long curls swirling through the air. Jack, Annie, and Florence all laughed at the sight.

Finally the countess put Koku on her shoulder and looked at Jack and Annie. "Oh, my!" she cried. "What happened to you?"

"Koku ran away from jackals," said Florence. "And they rescued her from the top of a cliff."

"Oh, my dear children, thank you!" said the

countess. "Koku, you little rascal, causing these nice children to suffer so!"

"We'll be fine," said Annie. "Miss Nightingale has taken really good care of us."

"Well, you are the best baby baboon caretakers in the world!" said the countess. "I would love to stay and admire you all day. But we must hurry away. Our boat is leaving for Cairo! Say good-bye, Koku. Say thank you to your wonderful friends!"

Koku looked at Jack and Annie. Her dark eyes were soft and grateful. *Uhh-woh,* she said.

"Uhh-woh," Annie answered.

"Good-bye, Koku von Kensky," said Jack, waving with his left hand.

"Farewell!" said the countess. Then she and the baby baboon headed out the door.

CHAPTER TEN

Good-Bye, Thebes!

"I'm afraid we should leave, too," said Annie. "It's almost time for us to meet up with our parents."

"Oh, yes, of course," said Florence. "Where do you need to go?"

"Across the Nile," said Jack, "by the sycamore. We'll rendezvous there." Jack put on his shirt, his belt, and his hat.

"Good," said Florence. "No doubt Mustafa and Ali are already sitting by the river, waiting to help travelers. We will shout for him to row across and pick you up."

"Thanks," said Jack.

"And you will need this, Annie," said Florence. She went to a small closet and took out a wooden crutch. "I always travel with a few medical supplies. It's not much, but it should help you a bit."

"Great!" said Annie. She took the crutch from Florence and used it to help herself down from the bed.

Jack climbed down, too, careful not to jostle his right arm. As they followed Florence out of her cabin, dawn was spreading its rosy glow across the Temple of Luxor, the anchored sailboats, and the waters of the Nile.

Charles and Selina were already on the deck. Selina was sketching the temple, while Charles sat in a deck chair, reading a book. "Good morning!" they both exclaimed when they saw Jack, Annie, and Florence.

"Say good morning *and* good-bye to our new friends," said Florence. "Jack and Annie are leaving Thebes soon."

"Oh, dear, we will miss these brave American

children," said Selina. She put down her sketching tools and rushed over to give Jack and Annie careful hugs. "Good luck with your injuries, my dears."

"Thanks," said Jack.

"Thanks for helping us," said Annie.

"Good-bye, old chap," said Charles, shaking Jack's left hand. "And, young lady, I'm sure you'll be leaping over barrels soon."

"Righto," said Annie.

Donkeys brayed across the river.

"Look!" said Jack, pointing to Mustafa and Ali on the western bank.

"They are already up and ready for work," said Charles. The Englishman stepped across the boat deck, faced the Nile, and shouted, "Mustafa!" He waved for the guide to come across the river.

Mustafa climbed into his rowboat, pushed off the bank, and started rowing across.

"Come," said Florence. "I'll accompany you to the water's edge."

"Thanks again!" said Annie, waving good-bye to Charles and Selina.

Charles tipped his hat as Selina waved back. Then Jack and Annie followed Florence down the landing. In the glowing dawn light, a heron was standing on one leg in the water. "He looks like me," said Annie, hopping on one foot.

Florence smiled. "There is more activity here

in the first hour of cool morning than at any other time of day," she said.

Men in robes and turbans were sitting under a palm tree, smoking a water pipe. Two women were bathing small children in the Nile. Some girls were spreading wet clothes over rocks to dry.

Jack heard someone shouting. He and Annie and Florence turned to look back at the sailboats anchored offshore. Lord and Lady Bickerson were on the deck of one of the boats. They were swatting and yelling at the flies.

"Poor souls," breathed Florence.

"The flies?" asked Annie.

Florence laughed. "I like you both very much," she said. "I think we could be good friends."

"I think so, too," said Annie.

"Me too," Jack added. His whole opinion of Florence had changed since she had tended to their injuries so kindly and he had heard her speak about her dreams.

"Ah, here is your carriage," said Florence.

Mustafa had arrived in his rowboat. He pulled it ashore. Then he and Florence helped Annie and Jack climb aboard and take their seats.

"Good-bye, Jack and Annie," Florence said, standing on the riverbank. "You must visit me if you ever come to England."

Jack was sad to leave her, and even sadder to think they would probably never see her again. "Good luck with everything," he said. "Hold on to your dreams."

"We'll miss you," said Annie.

Florence smiled her most radiant smile and waved. Then she turned and walked away.

Mustafa used his oars to push off, then began rowing back across the River Nile. Geese flew overhead. A pelican was perched on the crocodile's rock. The old Egyptian sang his song. The words were still impossible to understand, but Jack felt he knew what they meant now. They celebrated the Nile and all the life around it—ancient and new, beasts and birds.

When they came to the other side of the river, Mustafa pulled the rowboat up onto the bank, then helped Jack and Annie climb out. Nearby, Ali was talking to some travelers who wanted donkeys. He called to his grandfather.

"Wait, please," said Jack. He fumbled in his

pouch for their Egyptian money. He pulled out their coins and offered them to Mustafa. "These are all for you, please. You helped us a lot. You saved us, actually."

The guide shook his head. "No," he said. It was the first word Jack had heard him speak. "I helped you not for money, but because you needed help. It would be wrong for me to accept payment for a simple good deed."

"Oh, yes. I understand," said Jack. He put away his coins. "Thank you very much."

"Yes, thank you," said Annie. "And please tell Ali good-bye from us."

The old man nodded, silent again, and headed toward his grandson and the new travelers. *Day after day, Mustafa and Ali help people,* Jack thought, *and always with gentleness and dignity.*

"Come on, let's go, quick," Annie said, "while no one's looking."

"Righto!" said Jack.

Using her crutch, Annie hobbled to the syca-more tree. Jack followed her. When they slipped under the canopy of spreading branches, Annie grabbed the rope ladder.

"Oh, man, can you climb up with your sprained ankle?" Jack asked her.

"No big deal," she said. "But what about you, with your hurt shoulder and arm?"

"No big deal," said Jack.

Annie propped her crutch against the tree trunk. Then she grabbed the sides of the ladder and stepped with her good foot onto the bottom rung. Moving slowly and carefully, she started up to the top. "Oww . . . oww . . . oww," she said under her breath as she climbed.

Jack watched as Annie pulled herself inside the tree house. Then he grabbed a rung of the ladder with his left hand. *At least this sycamore tree isn't as tall as the oak tree in Frog Creek,* he thought. Keeping his right arm still, he slowly pulled himself up, teetering this way and that on the rope ladder. Finally he painfully heaved himself into the tree house, too. He was exhausted. He had no idea how they were going to climb back down.

"Ready to go?" Annie asked. She had already opened the Pennsylvania book to the picture of Frog Creek.

Jack sighed. "Yeah, but I don't know how we're going to explain your ankle and my shoulder to Mom and Dad."

"We'll solve that problem when we get home," said Annie. She pointed at the picture. "I wish we could go *there*! Good-bye, Thebes!"

The wind started to blow.

The tree house started to spin.

It spun faster and faster.

Then everything was still.

Absolutely still.

Jack's arm sling was gone. He moved his shoulder carefully. The pain was gone, too! He breathed a huge sigh of relief. He was happy to be wearing his own clothes again, and even happier that his arm and shoulder were perfectly fine.

"No more bandage!" said Annie. "No more sprained ankle!"

Jack and Annie looked at each other in wonder. "Cool," they said together.

"I guess what happens in Thebes stays in Thebes," said Jack.

Annie laughed.

"Okay! We have the third secret of greatness now," said Jack. He took out his pencil and picked up the piece of paper from the floor. Under the words *humility* and *hard work*, he added,

meaning and purpose

"Isn't that two secrets?" said Annie.

"No, in this case, I think it takes two words to say one thing really well," said Jack.

"I'm glad to know Florence's life will have meaning and purpose," said Annie. "I didn't want to tell her this and freak her out, but she'll go to nursing school in Germany. And she'll be a great nurse in the Crimea, and eventually she'll be the founder of modern nursing."

"Whew," said Jack.

"Yeah, *whew*," said Annie.

"And you know who else I think had meaning and purpose in his life?" said Jack.

"Who?" said Annie.

"Mustafa," said Jack. "He worked so hard. But he wouldn't take money for doing the right thing. And I could tell he really loved his grandson."

"That's true!" said Annie. "Mustafa's life definitely had meaning and purpose."

"I'll bet Ali grows up to be just like him," said Jack. He took the tiny bottle of mist from his pack and put it on the paper. Then he looked at Annie. "Your ring, m'lady."

"Oh, I forgot," she said. She pulled the Ring of Truth off her finger and put it on the paper next to the bottle.

"Okay! Let's go home," said Jack.

"I'm ready," said Annie. She led the way down the ladder.

Jack followed. "Wow," he said. "This ladder is a lot easier without a hurt shoulder and a sprained ankle, isn't it?"

"No kidding!" said Annie.

Jack and Annie started walking together through the Frog Creek woods.

"Hey, do you think *our* lives have meaning and purpose?" said Annie.

"I guess so . . . ," said Jack. "We help people."

"And animals," said Annie. "Horses, pandas, penguins, polar bears, dogs, elephants, kangaroos, koalas, baby baboons—"

"I'll tell you one thing," Jack interrupted. "Right now, my life has only *one* purpose."

"What's that?" asked Annie.

"To go home, sit on the front porch, read my book, take notes, and drink lemonade," said Jack.

"Home, sweet home," said Annie.

"Home, sweet home," repeated Jack.

And he and Annie hurried home through the summery, good-smelling, bird-singing, shadowy Frog Creek woods.

Author's Note

Florence Nightingale traveled through Egypt as a tourist in 1849 and 1850 with her friends Selina and Charles Bracebridge. At that time, she was confused about what she should do with her life. Her wealthy, upper-class family wanted her to marry and become "a proper society lady," but Florence wanted to help others and become a professional nurse. In those days, very few women worked in hospitals, and if they did, they were treated as maids.

While traveling on the Nile, Florence became convinced that she should follow her dreams. On her way home, she visited an institute in Germany that taught nursing practices. Soon after, she trained at the institute, then got a job in London working as a nurse.

A few years later, Florence became famous for her heroic medical work during the Crimean War on the Black Sea. She returned to England and spent the rest of her long life working to help others by improving conditions in hospitals, organizing patient care practices, and training nurses. Today it is often said that Florence Nightingale invented modern nursing.

Mary Pope Osborne

Turn the page for a sneak peek at *Magic Tree House Fact Tracker: Heroes for All Times*

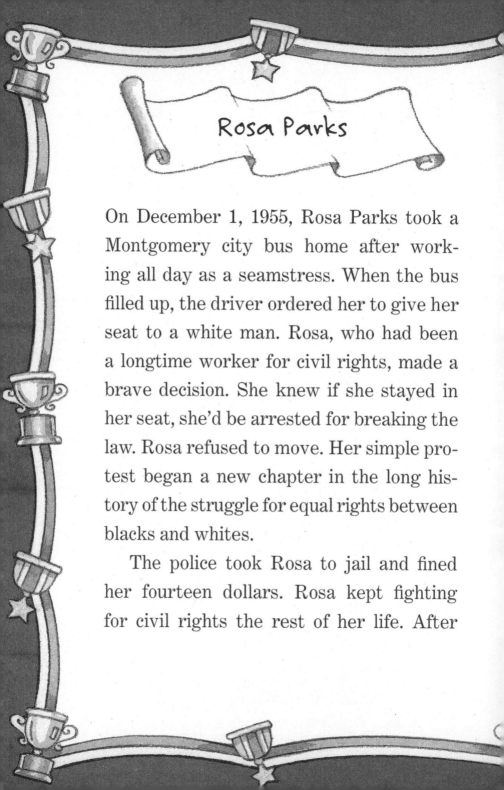

Rosa Parks

On December 1, 1955, Rosa Parks took a Montgomery city bus home after working all day as a seamstress. When the bus filled up, the driver ordered her to give her seat to a white man. Rosa, who had been a longtime worker for civil rights, made a brave decision. She knew if she stayed in her seat, she'd be arrested for breaking the law. Rosa refused to move. Her simple protest began a new chapter in the long history of the struggle for equal rights between blacks and whites.

The police took Rosa to jail and fined her fourteen dollars. Rosa kept fighting for civil rights the rest of her life. After she died in 2005, her coffin was brought to the U.S. Capitol so that people could pass by and pay their respects. She was the first woman ever to have this honor. Today Rosa is known as the mother of the civil rights movement.

Coming in May 2014!

Don't miss Jack and Annie's soccer
adventure at the 1970 World Soccer Cup
in Mexico City!

Score a GOOOALLL with Jack and Annie!

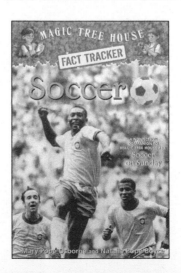